THIS WALKER BOOK BELONGS TO:

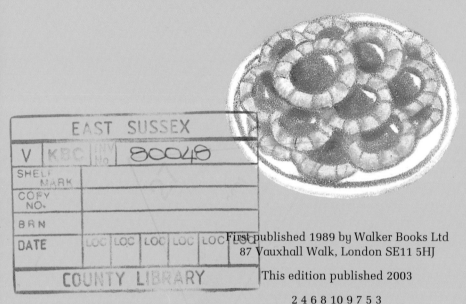

First published 1989 by Walker Books Ltd
87 Vauxhall Walk, London SE11 5HJ

This edition published 2003

2 4 6 8 10 9 7 5 3

© 1989 Anthony Browne

The right of Anthony Browne to be identified as
author/illustrator of this work has been asserted by him
in accordance with the Copyright, Designs and Patents Act 1988

This book has been typeset in Melior Educational

Printed in China

British Library Cataloguing in Publication Data:
a catalogue record for this book is available from the British Library

ISBN 0-7445-9858-3

www.walkerbooks.co.uk

Things I Like

ANTHONY BROWNE

WALKER BOOKS

AND SUBSIDIARIES

LONDON · BOSTON · SYDNEY · AUCKLAND

This is me
and this is what I like:

Painting ...

and riding my bike.

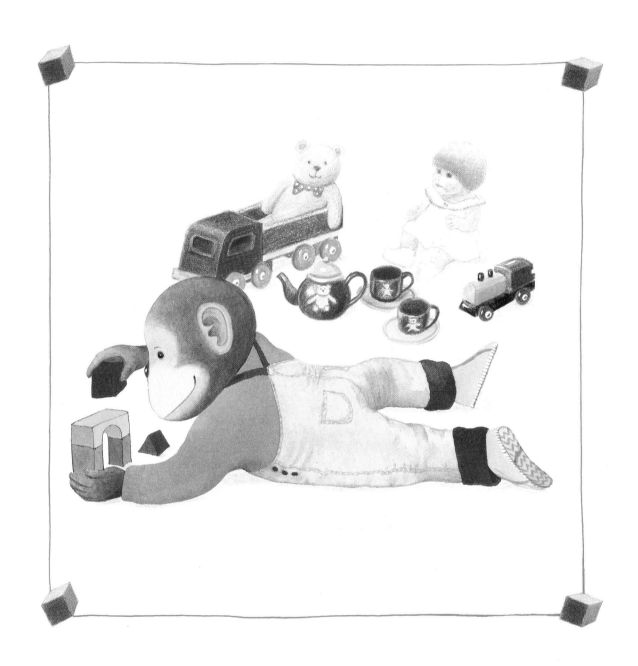

Playing with toys ...

and dressing up.

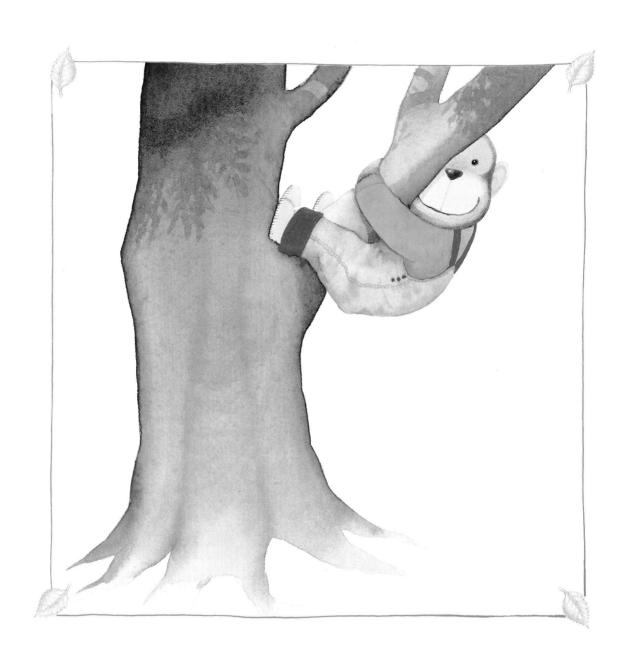

Climbing trees ...

and kicking a ball.

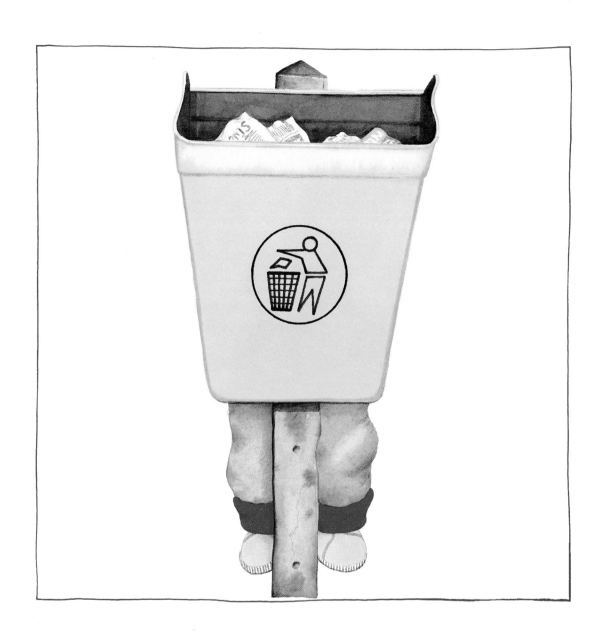

Hiding ...

and acrobatics.

Building sand-castles ...

and paddling in the sea.

Making a cake ...

and watching TV.

Going to birthday parties ...

and being with my friends.

Having a bath ...

hearing a bedtime story ...

and dreaming.

WALKER BOOKS is the world's leading
independent publisher of children's books.
Working with the best authors and illustrators
we create books for all ages, from babies
to teenagers – books your child will
grow up with and always remember. So…

FOR THE BEST CHILDREN'S BOOKS,
LOOK FOR THE BEAR